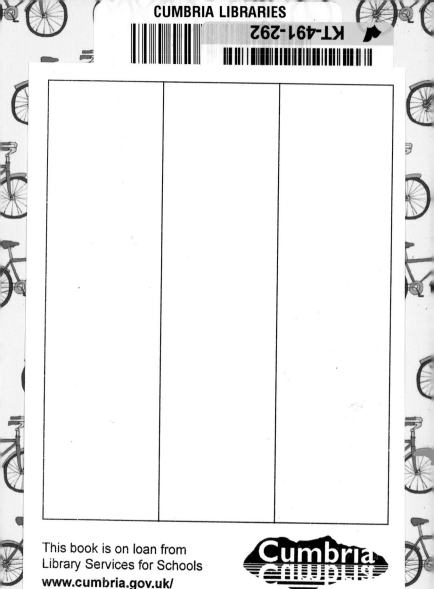

This book is on loan from
Library Services for Schools
www.cumbria.gov.uk/
libraries/schoolslibserv

Cumbria
County Council

First published in 2019 in Great Britain by
Barrington Stoke Ltd
18 Walker Street, Edinburgh, EH3 7LP

www.barringtonstoke.co.uk

Text © 2019 Jonathan Meres
Illustrations © 2019 Hannah Coulson

A CIP catalogue record for this book is available
from the British Library upon request

ISBN: 978-1-78112-869-5

Printed in China by Leo

This book is in a super readable format for young
readers beginning their independent reading journey.

JONATHAN MERES

Special Delivery

With illustrations by
Hannah Coulson

Barrington Stoke

To Charlie, Cara and Lucy

CONTENTS

Chapter 1
Toast

It was breakfast time. Frank had just taken a bite of toast. But before he took another, there was something he needed to say.

"Mum?"

"Yes, love?" said Frank's mum.

"I want a new bike."

Frank's mum looked up from her iPad. "Really?" she said.

Frank nodded.

"What's wrong with the one you've got?" his mum asked.

"It's too small," said Frank.

Frank's mum frowned.

"Can't you just raise the seat up a bit?" she said.

Frank thought for a moment. His mum was right. He could just raise the seat up a bit. But he didn't want to. What he wanted was a new bike. Why did grown-ups always have to be so boring? It wasn't fair.

"Well?" said Frank's mum. "Can't you?"

"Yes, I can," Frank said. "But I've had my bike for about seventy-eight years!"

Someone laughed. Frank turned around. His sister, Lottie, was standing in the doorway. She was back from doing her paper round.

"What's so funny?" said Frank.

"You're only nine," replied Lottie.

"So?" said Frank.

"So, how can you have had your bike for seventy-eight years?" said Lottie.

Frank sighed. It wasn't only grown-ups who were boring. Big sisters could be boring, too.

"Your brother wants a new one," Frank's mum said.

Lottie sat down.

"You do know bikes cost a lot of money, don't you?" Frank's mum said.

"Course I do," Frank replied.

"And you know that money doesn't grow on trees?"

"Course I know that," Frank said. "That's just what people say."

"Is it your birthday soon?" said Frank's mum.

Frank shook his head. What a strange question. Had his mum forgotten when his birthday was?

"Is Christmas just around the corner?"

Frank shook his head again. Christmas wasn't just around the corner. Didn't his mum know anything?

"In that case," said Frank's mum, "we have a problem, don't we?"

"Unless ..." began Lottie.

"Unless what?" Frank said.

"Well, it's just an idea," Lottie said. "But you could help me do my paper round."

Frank didn't understand.

"Why would I do that?" he said.

"So that I could pay you, silly!" said Lottie.

"Pay me?" Frank said.

"It wouldn't be much," said Lottie. "But it would be a start."

"That's very kind of you, Lottie," said Frank's mum. "Isn't it, Frank?"

"Yes, but ..." Frank began.

"But what?" said his mum.

"It will take at least a thousand years to save up enough for a bike!"

Lottie laughed.

"Perhaps you wouldn't have to save up *all* the money," said Frank's mum.

Frank frowned.

"What do you mean, Mum?" he said.

"I mean, let's wait and see what happens," said Frank's mum.

"Well?" said Lottie.

"I'll do it," said Frank.

"Great," said Lottie. "I'll wake you at six."

"What?" Frank said. "Six o'clock? In the morning?"

"Of course!" Lottie laughed. "Do you want a new bike or not?"

Frank wanted a new bike more than he'd ever wanted anything before. And if that meant getting up at six o'clock the next morning, then that's what he'd have to do.

"Well?" said Lottie.

"See you at six," said Frank.

"Excellent!" said his mum. "Now eat that toast before it gets cold!"

Chapter 2
On Your Marks!

Lottie woke Frank at six o'clock the next day. Frank got dressed and had some juice. Then he and Lottie cycled to the newsagents. There was nobody else around. Even the birds had only just started singing.

Frank waited outside the newsagents while Lottie collected the papers.

He didn't mind being up so early. It was the summer holidays. It was bright and sunny. In the winter, it would still have been cold and dark at this time.

Lottie carried the delivery bag at the start of the round. It was too heavy for Frank. But even Lottie wobbled a bit as she set off down the road on her bike.

"Hey! Wait for me!" cried Frank, pedalling after his sister as fast as he could.

"No!" yelled Lottie. "You'll just have to keep up!"

Frank didn't think that was very fair. Lottie had a big bike. His was only tiny. But then, that was why he was doing this. So he could get a brand-new one!

Frank skidded to a halt outside the first house. He got off his bike and leaned it against the wall. Lottie was already marching up the path. Frank ran after her.

"What's the hurry?" he panted.

"People don't like to be kept waiting for their newspapers," said Lottie.

"I see," said Frank.

"Now pay attention," said Lottie. "The number of the house is written here."

Lottie was pointing at a number four. It was written in pen in the top

right-hand corner of the newspaper.
And the number on the door of the house
was also four.

"See?" said Lottie.

Frank nodded. "Number four," he
said.

"Excellent," said Lottie. "Now watch."

Frank watched as Lottie folded the
newspaper and then pushed it through
the letterbox.

There was a soft thump as it landed on the other side.

"Any questions?" said Lottie.

"Yes," said Frank. "Can I do the next one, please?"

Lottie grinned. "Of course you can."

"Come on, slowcoach!" said Frank, marching back down the path.

Now it was Lottie's turn to catch up.

"Hey, wait for me!" she laughed.

Chapter 3
Beware of the Donkey

When they got to the next house, Frank checked the number on the newspaper. It was the same as the number on the door. Number six. Frank folded the newspaper and pushed it through the letterbox. There was a soft thump as it landed on the other side. A moment later, there was a barking sound.

"They've got a dog," explained Lottie.

"Oh, really?" grinned Frank. "I thought it was a donkey."

Lottie looked at Frank and smiled.

"Very funny, Frank."

Frank delivered the next newspaper. And the next one. And the next one, too. Before long, the bag was light enough for him to carry.

He wobbled about a bit on his bike.

But he soon got the hang of it.

"This way," said Lottie as they turned into another street.

It was a very long street. At the end of it was a very grand-looking entrance. There was no number. Just a sign that said, "Riverside Court".

"Wow!" said Frank. "Who lives here?"

"Wait and see," Lottie said.

They cycled down a long, twisting driveway to a big house. It was modern and made of red bricks. Frank thought it looked much too big for just one family to live in. And he was right. It was.

"This is sheltered accommodation," said Lottie.

"What does that mean?" said Frank.

"Flats for elderly people," Lottie replied.

"Oh," said Frank. "So, *lots* of people live here!"

"Exactly," Lottie said as she pressed a button. A moment later, there was a buzzing sound. She opened the door.

Chapter 4
"Howdy, Pardners!"

Inside Riverside Court, everything was calm and peaceful.

Pictures of mountains and waterfalls hung on the walls. The smell of bacon and coffee filled the air. Gentle music hummed from one flat. The chatter of breakfast television mumbled from another.

The corridors were covered in soft carpet. Frank and Lottie hardly made a sound as they padded along, delivering newspapers.

"This is really cool," Frank said.

"Wait till you see this," Lottie said.

"Wait till I see what?" Frank said.

They turned a corner.

"This," said Lottie.

In front of them was a bright yellow door. A horseshoe was nailed to it, just above the number.

On the wall next to the door was a poster from an old movie. A cowboy was galloping along on a horse. There was a cloud of dust.

It looked very exciting.

Underneath the poster was a table. On the table was a small statue of a cowboy on a horse. The horse was standing on its back legs. Its front hooves were waving in the air. The cowboy was waving, too.

And on the ground in front of the door was a doormat. It had the words "Howdy, Pardner!" written on it in big black letters.

"Wow!" said Frank. "I wonder who lives here."

Lottie gave a shrug. "I don't know," she said. "Amazing, isn't it?"

They stood in silence for a few moments.

"Well?" Lottie said at last.

"What?" said Frank.

"Are you just going to stand there all day, or are you going to deliver the paper?"

"Oh, yes," Frank laughed. "I almost forgot!"

Frank reached into the bag and took out a paper.

"It's the last one!" he said.

"That's right," replied Lottie. "It's always the last one. Then we can go home."

Frank folded the newspaper and pushed it through the letterbox. But this time, there was no thump. A moment later, the door opened. A face peered out.

"Yee-haw!" said an old lady, waving the newspaper in the air. "I thought I heard voices."

"Hello," said Lottie.

"Hello," said Frank.

"Howdy, pardners!" said the old lady.

"We were just delivering your paper," Lottie explained.

"How marvellous," said the old lady. "Thank you so much!"

"Are you a cowboy?" Frank asked.

The old lady laughed. Behind her glasses, her eyes sparkled.

"No, dear. I wish I was. But I'm not. I'm just a silly old lady."

Frank frowned.

"I don't think you're silly at all," he said. "I think you're cool."

The old lady seemed surprised.

"Do you really?" she said.

Frank nodded.

"Definitely," he said. "And I love all these things outside your flat."

"You're most kind," the old lady said.

"I mean it," said Frank.

The old lady smiled. "Well, I mustn't keep you," she said. "Goodbye."

"Goodbye," said Lottie.

"Goodbye," said Frank.

"Yee-haw!" said the old lady.

"Yee-haw!" said Frank and Lottie together as the old lady closed the door.

Lottie turned to Frank and smiled.

"Well, that was a surprise!" she said.

Frank nodded. It wasn't every day you met someone who spoke like a cowboy.

"Same time tomorrow?" said Lottie.

Frank didn't even have to think about it.

"Definitely."

"Excellent," said Lottie. "Time for breakfast!"

Chapter 5
Circles

Frank helped Lottie on her paper round the next day. And the next day. And the day after that. He soon knew exactly where to go and exactly what to do. Frank said he could probably do it with his eyes closed if he wanted to. Lottie said she didn't think that was a very good idea, because he might fall off his bike. They laughed.

One day, when they'd finished their round and had eaten breakfast, Frank and Lottie went to the park.

They played football for a while. Then they went on the swings, like they used to when they were little.

Then some of Lottie's friends turned up. After that, Lottie just wanted to talk to them. Frank soon got bored. So he went for a walk by himself.

Frank hadn't gone far when he saw someone heading towards him.

Someone with a big hat. And a waistcoat. And a red silk scarf with white spots. And pointy boots with a fancy pattern on them. Frank thought he knew who it was.

"Howdy, pardner!" said a voice.

Frank was right. He *did* know who it was. It was the old lady from Riverside Court.

"Hello," he said.

"Yee-haw!" said the old lady.

"Yee-haw," replied Frank. Because he didn't want to be rude.

The old lady looked at Frank for a moment. "Do I know you?" she asked.

Frank nodded. "I deliver your newspaper."

"Do you really?" said the old lady. "How marvellous! That's most kind of you."

"Well, not just me," Frank said. "Me and my sister."

"Your sister?" said the old lady.

"Yes," Frank said. "Lottie."

The old lady looked surprised. "Lottie?" she said.

Frank nodded again.

"How odd!" said the old lady. "I have a sister called Lottie, too!"

"Do you?" Frank replied. "That's funny."

"Yes, it is," the old lady said. "We live on Primrose Avenue! Number thirty-seven."

Frank wasn't sure what to say. He knew that the old lady didn't live on Primrose Avenue. Wherever that was. And it was strange that she didn't remember meeting him before. It was only a few days ago.

"Have you seen her?" the old lady asked.

"Who?" said Frank.

"Lottie."

"Your sister?"

"Of course," the old lady said. "Why? Do you know someone else called Lottie?"

"Yes," Frank said. "*My* sister."

"You have a sister called Lottie?" the old lady said. "Well I never! So do I!"

Frank smiled. He didn't know what else to do. The conversation was going round in circles.

"There you are! I didn't know where you'd gone," said a voice.

Frank turned around. Lottie was walking towards them.

"Yee-haw!" said the old lady.

"Yee-haw," said Lottie.

The old lady looked at Lottie for a moment.

"Do I know you?" she said.

Lottie nodded.

"I deliver your newspaper," she replied.

"Do you really?" said the old lady.

"Yes," said Lottie. "We chatted the other day."

"Of course we did," the old lady said. "I'm such a silly billy sometimes!"

"I love your outfit by the way," said Lottie.

"Me too," said Frank. "It's cool!"

"Do you think so?" the old lady said.

"Definitely!" Frank said. "It makes you look like a real cowboy!"

The old lady looked very pleased.

"Thank you," she said. "That's awfully kind. I wish I really was one."

"A cowboy?" Frank said.

The old lady nodded.

"Lottie and I go to see cowboy films all the time!" she said.

"Lottie?" said Lottie. "That's my name, too!"

"Your name's Lottie?" said the old
lady.

Lottie nodded.

"How funny!" the old lady said. "That's my sister's name, too!"

Frank looked at the old lady. He'd already told her twice that he had a sister called Lottie. But he didn't say anything, because she was very nice and, again, he didn't want to be rude.

"Well, I must be getting home, I suppose," the old lady said. "Lottie will be expecting me."

Frank thought for a moment. He had a feeling that the old lady might be lost. He knew that he had to do something. They couldn't just leave her wandering around.

"We're going that way," he said. "We can come with you, if you like?"

"To Primrose Avenue?" said the old lady. "Thank you so much. That's most kind."

Lottie looked puzzled. "Primrose Avenue?" she said. "But you live at ..."

"Ssshhh!" said Frank, putting a finger up to his mouth. "I'll explain later."

Chapter 6
"Yee-haw!"

"*There* you are, Mother!" said a voice.

Frank, Lottie and the old lady had just arrived at Riverside Court. A man was walking up the drive towards them.

"Oh, hello, dear," said the old lady.

"I've been looking everywhere for you," he said.

"Oh, there's no need to worry about me, dear," said the old lady. "This charming young man has been looking after me. We've had a lovely time chatting about cowboys."

"Thank you so much," the man said to Frank. "My mother gets a little confused from time to time."

"Do I?" said the old lady. "Oh yes, that's right. I do."

The man smiled at Frank.

"What's your name?" he said.

"Frank," said Frank. "And this is my sister, Lottie."

"Hi," said Lottie.

"Lottie?" said the old lady. "I have a sister called Lottie, too! We live at 37 Primrose Avenue."

"No, Mother," said the man in a gentle voice. "You *used* to live on Primrose Avenue. You live here now. At Riverside Court. Remember?"

"Of course," said the old lady. "I'm such a silly billy sometimes."

"How did you know my mother lives here?" the man asked.

"We deliver her newspaper," replied Lottie.

"I see," said the man.

"I'm saving up for a new bike," Frank said.

"A new bike?" said the old lady. "How marvellous!"

"Yes," said Frank. "But they cost a lot of money. And money doesn't grow on trees, you know. That's just what people say."

The man smiled.

"And it's not my birthday soon," Frank continued. "And Christmas isn't just around the corner."

"Well, thanks again," said the man. "I can tell that my mother has really enjoyed talking to you."

"Oh, I have," the old lady said. "You must come and have tea one day."

"I'd love to," said Frank.

"And bring your sister!"

Frank nodded. "I will."

The old lady thought for a moment.

"What's your name again, dear?"

"Lottie," said Lottie.

"Lottie," the old lady said. "Of course. How could I forget that?"

"Come along now, Mother," said the man as he opened the door. "Let's get you home."

"My name is Mary by the way!" said the old lady as she disappeared inside.

"Bye, Mary!" called Frank.

Mary waved.

"Yee-haw!" she called.

Frank waved back.

"Yee-haw," he said.

Chapter 7
An Extra-Special Delivery

It was the next morning. Frank was sitting at the table, munching toast.

"So?" his mum said. "Are you enjoying it?"

Frank frowned.

"Enjoying what?" he said. "My toast?"

Frank's mum laughed.

"No," she said. "I mean, are you enjoying doing the paper round?"

"Oh," Frank said. "Yes. I love it. It's fun."

"That's good," his mum said. "Perhaps you can take over one day."

"What do you mean, Mum?" said Frank.

"Well, Lottie's not going to do it for ever, is she?"

Frank thought about that. His mum was right. Lottie wasn't going to keep delivering newspapers for ever. One day, someone else was going to do it instead. And that someone could be him.

"Think of all the money you could save if you did!" Frank's mum said.

Frank thought about that, too.

His mum was right again. He could save so much money, he'd be able to buy a different bike for each day of the week!

"Was someone talking about money?" said a voice.

Frank turned around. Lottie was standing in the doorway. "This is for you," she said.

Frank watched his sister. As if by magic, she pulled a ten-pound note from her pocket.

"Really?" he said.

Lottie laughed. "I can keep it if you want?"

Frank's mum looked at Frank.

"You've earned it, love," she said.

Frank took the ten-pound note from Lottie. "Wow!" he said. "Thanks!"

"There's something else for you," said Lottie. She held out an envelope.

"What is it?" Frank asked.

"I don't know," replied Lottie. "Open it and find out."

Frank took the envelope and opened it. There was a piece of paper inside. It was folded up. Frank unfolded it. It was a letter. He began to read.

Dear Frank,

Thank you, once again, for everything that you and your sister did yesterday. You were very kind and understanding. As I said, my mother sometimes gets a little confused. But it was lovely to hear her talking about her old house and her sister. I never knew Aunt Lottie. She died a long time before I was born.

Here's a little something to put towards your new bike. You deserve it, for making an extra-special delivery!

Very best wishes,
Richard Smith

Frank finished reading the letter and looked in the envelope. He could hardly believe his eyes.

"Oh my goodness!" he said.

Frank put his hand inside the envelope and pulled out some money. There were two ten-pound notes.

"Twenty pounds?" he said. "Plus ten. That means I've got *thirty* pounds already!"

Frank's mum smiled.

"Yes, and just think," she said. "If you do the paper round for another seven weeks, you'll have one hundred pounds!"

"Wow!" said Frank again. It was hard to imagine having that much money. But he was doing his best.

"And if I give you *another* fifty," said Frank's mum, "you'll have one hundred and *fifty* pounds."

Now Frank couldn't believe his ears. So *that* was what his mum had meant when she said that he might not have to save up *all* the money for a new bike!

"What do you think?" said Frank's mum.

It was a good question. And Frank knew what the answer was.

"Well, Frank?" said Lottie.

Frank smiled.

"I think this is the best day *ever*," he said.

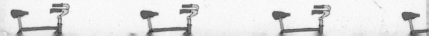